Harriet Dancing

Ruth Symes

Illustrated by

Caroline Jayne Church

Every morning Harriet ate four strawberries and one worm for breakfast and then she went to visit her best friend, Ivor.

For my husband Eric and
beautiful niece Jasmine
RS

For little Ella
CJC

© 2008 The Chicken House

First published in the United Kingdom in 2008 by
The Chicken House, 2 Palmer Street, Frome, Somerset, BA11 1DS
www.doublecluck.com

Text © 2008 Ruth Louise Symes
Illustrations © 2008 Caroline Jayne Church

Designed by Ian Butterworth

Printed and bound in Singapore by Imago

British Library Cataloguing in Publication Data available
Library of Congress Cataloguing in Publication data available

HB ISBN: 978-1-905294-36-7

PB ISBN: 978-1-905294-58-9

Harriet went over Frog's stream.

And to smell the forest flowers.

Lovely.

'I'm off to see Ivor today, hooray.
I wonder what games we will play, hooray.'

Suddenly
Harriet saw
hundreds of butterflies
dancing in the sunshine.

They looked so beautiful that
Harriet started to dance too.

She danced and she danced and she danced.

Twist and turn and skip and hop.

That way and this way.

This way and that way.

Spin around until you stop!

Dancing Harriet was the happiest hedgehog in the whole world.

Then Harriet noticed that
the butterflies had stopped
dancing, and were sitting in
the trees instead. Harriet was
dancing all alone.

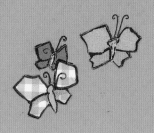

'Dance with me,' Harriet said.
But the butterflies didn't want to.

'The butterfly dance is only
for butterflies,' they said.
'Not hedgehogs.'

'Come on,' said Harriet.
'Just spin around and around like me.'

But the butterflies wouldn't.

'Butterflies only dance with
butterflies,' they said.

'Oh,'
said Harriet
in a small voice.
She felt very sad.

Oh.

Harriet
hurried away
as fast as she
could, so the
butterflies
wouldn't see
that she was
crying.

Harriet was crying so much she didn't look where she was going, and ended up rolling down a hill.

'Oh! Oh! Oh!' said Harriet and she curled up tight in a ball

so she wouldn't
hurt herself.

'Hello, Harriet,' said Ivor,
when Harriet knocked on his door.
'You're very late today.
Where've you been?'

'Dancing with the butterflies,' said Harriet.
'They looked like flowers dancing in the sky.'

'You look like a flower too,' said Ivor.

Then he showed Harriet her
reflection in a puddle.

Harriet smiled, but she still felt sad.
'The butterflies said I couldn't dance
with them,' she said.

'Then I'll dance with you instead,' said Ivor, and he curled up in a ball and rolled over and over in the flowers, until he was covered in petals too.

'We'll dance with you, Harriet,' said Rabbit and Mole and Frog.

Harriet and her friends danced and danced. Dancing Harriet was the happiest hedgehog in the whole world.

Twist and turn and skip and hop.
This way and that way.
That way and this way.
Spin around until you stop!

And as Harriet and her friends danced,

first one butterfly

and then another butterfly

and then another, came to watch.

'Can we join in too, please?'
they said at last.

'Of course!' said Harriet.

Twist and turn and skip and hop.

This way and that way.

That way and this way.

Spin around until you stop!

Dancing's for everyone, big and small.
Dancing's for sharing with one and all.

THE END